THE
WAY
IT
WORKS

ALSO BY WILLIAM KOWALSKI:

Orca/Raven

The Barrio Kings (2010)

Something Noble (2012)

Just Gone (2013)

HarperCollins

Eddie's Bastard (1999)

Somewhere South of Here (2001)

The Adventures of Flash Jackson (2003)

The Good Neighbor (2004)

Thomas Allen Publishers

The Hundred Hearts (2013)

THE
WAY
IT
WORKS

WILLIAM KOWALSKI

RAVEN BOOKS
an imprint of
ORCA BOOK PUBLISHERS

Library and Archives Canada Cataloguing in Publication

Kowalski, William, 1970-
The way it works / written by William Kowalski.
(Rapid reads)

Issued also in an electronic format.
ISBN 978-1-55469-367-2

I. Title. II. Series: Rapid reads
PS8571.O985W39 2010   C813'.54   C2010-903655-7

First published in the United States, 2010
Library of Congress Control Number: 2010929177

Summary: A young bi-racial man, who suddenly finds
himself homeless, struggles to maintain his dignity and to
make his own place in the world. (RL 2.6)

*Orca Book Publishers is dedicated to preserving the environment and has
printed this book on Forest Stewardship Council® certified paper.*

Orca Book Publishers gratefully acknowledges the support for
its publishing programs provided by the following agencies:
the Government of Canada through the Canada Book Fund and the
Canada Council for the Arts, and the Province of British Columbia
through the BC Arts Council and the Book Publishing Tax Credit.

Design by Teresa Bubela
Cover photography by Getty Images

ORCA BOOK PUBLISHERS
PO Box 5626, Stn. B
Victoria, BC Canada
V8R 6S4

ORCA BOOK PUBLISHERS
PO Box 468
Custer, WA USA
98240-0468

www.orcabook.com
Printed and bound in Canada.

16 15 14 13 • 5 4 3 2

To my students at Nova Scotia
Community College

probably not = chắc là o

CHAPTER ONE

You probably think you can tell if someone is homeless just by looking at them. But you're wrong. You can't. Because not every homeless person looks like a bum. Take it from me. I'm an expert. Nothing in this world is as it seems.

Look at that guy over there. The one in the brown uniform, unloading boxes from the delivery truck. He looks clean. He has a job. Maybe not a great one, but it's a job. How much you think he makes? Minimum wage. Maybe a dollar more.

Well, you can't make it on minimum anymore. Not in this city.

So how does he get by? Maybe he lives with his parents. Maybe his wife has a job too. Or maybe he washed his face and hair in the bathroom of a McDonald's this morning. Maybe he sleeps in the back of his truck. You just don't know.

Here's another one. A well-dressed white lady, sitting on that bench over there. She's got a skirt suit and high heels on. There's a nice purse in her lap. She's all dainty, the way she eats out of that plastic container. Her pinky sticks out like she's at a tea party. You look at her and you think, *Rich*. Or at least comfortable.

But wait a minute. If she's so comfortable, why is she just sitting there on a bench downtown at nine thirty in the morning? Could be she's just killing time. Or maybe she has nowhere else to go. Maybe those clothes are the only nice things she owns.

Maybe she got that food out of a trash can, and she's trying to make it last, because she doesn't know where her next meal is coming from.

Or take this guy, now. A young, light-skinned black man. Maybe twenty-one, twenty-two years old, clean-cut, in good shape. Not a bad-looking guy. A little on the short side. He's wearing a beautiful suit and carrying a nice briefcase. His shoes are so shiny they hurt your eyes. He's bopping along the sidewalk like he owns the place. Full of self-confidence. A spring in his step. Looks like nothing can stop him. Like he's on his way to take over the world.

You would never know that this well-dressed young man slept in his car last night. Or that he can only afford to eat once a day. Or that he's been trying to get a job for the last six months, but no one will hire him.

How do I know all this?

Because that young black man is me.

I'm Walter Davis. I'm twenty years old. My moms and I moved to this city about a year ago. We didn't know anybody here. But there was lots of opportunity. Moms was already trained as a paralegal, and I was going to community college. This city was supposed to be a new start for us. A brand-new life. The beginning of something better.

And for a while, it was.

Things started out great. Moms got a job at an important law firm. She had to work hard, but the money was worth it. It was the first professional job she ever had. Before that, she was a waitress. This was a big step up.

We got an apartment in a decent part of the city. Not too much crime, no graffiti on the buildings. Little by little, we started getting all the things we dreamed of. Nice kitchen appliances. A set of furniture for the living room. A flat-screen TV. We even got a car. It was used, sure, but we didn't care. Our last car wasn't even from this century. Sometimes it didn't even work. Now we had a steel-gray 2000 Chevrolet Caprice. It ran like a dream.

We were coming up in the world.

For my twentieth birthday, right before I graduated, Moms gave me a present. It was a suit. But not just any suit. It was a pin-striped wool Turnbull & Asser. She also gave me a pair of Tanino Crisci shoes and an Underwood briefcase. It must have cost her thousands. I told her to take it all back. But she said she wanted me to look my best when I started going on job interviews. The world judges a man by how he looks, she said.

I don't think I ever saw my moms really happy until we moved here. And I was happy too. We had it rough for a long time. Happiness was a welcome change.

Then came the life-insurance exam.

Moms wanted some security for me, in case anything happened to her. She could get a good deal on a policy, but she had to go see a doctor first. No big deal, right?

Except the doctor found a spot on her lungs. "Oops," he said. "You better get that checked out."

So she did. There wasn't just one spot. There were more. It turned out to be advanced lung cancer. How did that happen? Moms didn't even smoke.

I'll make a long story short. I don't like feeling sorry for myself.

There was to be no life insurance. Soon, my moms was too sick to work. She lost her health insurance. I took care of her as best I could. She passed away in a public hospice, in a room full of other dying people. I was holding her hand.

At least I was there for her. Some folks in that place died alone.

I kept on trying to find a job. No one was interested. Times are tough.

Soon our building went co-op. I couldn't afford to buy in. They told me I had to leave.

I sold all the things we were so proud of: television, furniture, appliances. That gave me some cash. Not much though. Enough to get by for a couple of months.

I started looking for a new apartment. But guess what? Landlords don't want tenants who don't have a job. It's that simple. No job, no apartment. That's the way it works.

I moved the few things I still owned into the trunk of my car. The first night I had to sleep in the backseat, I vowed it would be the last.

But it wasn't.

Boom. Just like that, I was homeless.

It really is that easy to lose everything, all in the blink of an eye.

CHAPTER TWO

It's a beautiful morning in late May.

I start the day early. When you sleep in your car, you don't have much choice. The city starts moving before the sun comes up. Street cleaners, garbage trucks, the first of the early-morning commuter buses. If I'm parked in a busy spot, I have to move before 6:00 AM. or I get towed. Sometimes there's a cop rapping on my window, looking at me like I'm a potential bank robber. Move along, they say. I never give the cops any lip. I just do what I'm told. The last thing I need is trouble with the law.

Everything I own fits in my car. I have four changes of clothes, including my suit. I keep my toiletries ready to go in a little bag. That way I can dive into a washroom in a restaurant or something, get clean fast, and get out again before anyone notices I'm there.

What else do I have? Not much. A pillow and a couple of blankets. I have just one book: *The Seven Habits of Highly Effective People*. This is my Bible. I read it when I'm bored, scared, depressed or worried about my future. It reminds me that I can do anything I want. I've read this book twenty times. I plan to read it another twenty at least.

First thing, after I get cleaned up and dressed for the day, is to eat a breakfast burrito. I know a little place where I can get them cheap. I hate to spend the money, but you have to eat breakfast if you want energy.

Then I go to the postal center. I rent a mailbox there so I can have an address to put on my resumé. Can't get a job without an address. I can also get on the Internet there, to check my email and research new companies.

But I have another reason for going to the postal center.

She's a beautiful young black girl about my age, maybe a little younger. Gorgeous eyes, smooth skin. A smile like a sunrise. Exotic-looking, although I can't put my finger on why. She works behind the counter. Her name tag says *Yolanda*.

Today, just like always, I walk in and check my mailbox. Nothing. Yolanda is talking to an Asian lady at the counter. She's speaking a different language. Sounds like Chinese.

What is a black girl doing speaking Chinese?

I try not to look like I'm eavesdropping. I go over to the computer and check my email. I've got a few responses from some interviews last week. Nothing very promising. Oh well. Never give up. That's my motto.

I print out a few more copies of my résumé. Then I wait in line to pay for them.

The Asian lady leaves. Then it's my turn.

"Hi," Yolanda says. Real friendly. She leans forward, rests her chin on her hand. "How are you today?"

"Real good," I say. Then I swallow hard and decide to go for it. What the heck? I've been wanting to talk to this girl for weeks. It's not gonna happen unless I make it happen.

"Did I just hear you speaking Chinese?" I ask.

She smiles.

"Yes, you did," she says. "Mandarin, actually."

"And...you speak Mandarin why?"

"My mom is Chinese. I grew up speaking to her in Mandarin and to my dad in English."

11

"You're kidding," I say. "So, you're half Chinese and half black?"

"Yup."

"Wow. That's quite a mix."

"Sure is," she says.

"Me, I'm half black and half white," I tell her.

"Are those copies everything for today?"

Uh-oh. Maybe I've gone too far. She doesn't want to talk about this. I'm just one more customer, being too nosy. Better make a joke, then leave on a high note.

"Being mixed race sure can be interesting," I say. "I remember one time, I was in a store with my moms. The guy behind the counter whispers to her, 'Did you know there's a black guy following you around?' And she goes, 'Yeah, he's my son.'"

Yolanda laughs at that. Her teeth are perfect, like two rows of polished gems.

"Your mom is white?" she says.

"She passed away a little while ago."

"I'm sorry to hear that."

I give her a small bill from my precious stash. I carry my money on me at all times, in a big roll. This is partly for security. I don't trust banks. And it's partly because I like to flash a wad from time to time. It's a good way to impress people. Because would Yolanda be talking to me if she knew I was homeless? No way.

Yolanda gives me my change.

"You want something to put those copies in?" she says.

"Sure," I say.

She slides them into a paper bag. But first, I notice she peeks at them.

"Résumés, huh?" she says.

"Yeah. I'm doin' the job-hunt thing."

"What kind of job are you looking for?"

"Finance," I say. "Anything to do with finance. That's my field."

"Impressive," she says, smiling again.

13

"Thanks," I say. And then, before I even know what I'm doing, I say, "I'd love to take you out to dinner sometime. I think we'd have a lot of fun. What do you say?"

She looks at me like she can't believe what she just heard. I can't believe it either. I wasn't even planning on asking. It just slipped out.

"Dinner?" she says, real casual. "Sure. When?"

I make a big show of looking up at the ceiling, like I'm running through dates in my head. Then I smile.

"Tonight?" I say.

She shrugs.

"Okay," she says. "Let me write my address down for you."

CHAPTER THREE

Only after I leave the postal center do I realize what I've done. I've committed to picking Yolanda up in seven hours. But there's no way I can let her see my car. Not in the shape it's in. I have to clean it.

But first, I have to find someplace to put my stuff. And I still have my daily rounds to make. The world doesn't stop just because I have a date. I still need a job. I'm going to have to hurry to get everything done in time.

I go through the same routine, knocking on doors, sitting through interviews.

But it's the same old story. Either I don't have enough education, or they're just not hiring right now.

It would be easy to get upset. But I know I have to keep my head on straight. And I've got tonight to look forward to.

I decide to rent a locker at the bus station. Whatever doesn't fit in my trunk can go in there. Then I take the Caprice to a car wash. I spend forty bucks getting it cleaned, inside and out.

Forty dollars is a lot of money to me. When I sold all our stuff, I got about eight hundred bucks for it. That sounds like a fortune, but if that's all you've got, it's nothing. That money is the only thing keeping me from starving to death. I never spend money unless I have to. Not even on food. And now, not only am I dropping forty on the detailing, but I'm planning on paying for dinner for two. Today is easily going to cost me a hundred bucks.

But you know what? I don't care. A man has to live a little too. It's been a long time since I've been on a date.

I take a sponge bath in a public washroom in the downtown mall. I have to move fast. Security comes through here every twenty minutes, looking for guys just like me. Then I put my suit back on. I check myself in the mirror. I'm not thrilled with what I see. But there's no time to work miracles. I walk back out to my car and check the time. Five thirty. Half an hour to go.

I follow Yolanda's directions to her house. I'm early, so I drive around, checking out the neighborhood. It's nice. Working class, but respectable. There's a decent car in every driveway. A satellite dish on every roof. It's the kind of place I wouldn't mind living someday.

Who am I kidding? I'd live in a cardboard box, as long as I could call it mine.

thường lình, đúng
đột ngột

At six sharp I park in front of Yolanda's house. I've got some flowers I picked on the down low from a nearby park. No roses yet. It's too soon for that. And roses are expensive.

I knock on the door. I hear footsteps inside too heavy to be Yolanda's. The front door opens. There stands the largest black man I've ever seen in my life. I don't mean fat. I mean giant. He must be seven feet tall. He's as wide as a tree trunk. And he's not smiling.

"Good evening," he says.

"Uh…hello, sir," I say. "I must have the wrong house."

"You looking for Yolanda?"

"Yes, sir."

"Then you don't have the wrong house. Baby! Somebody at the door for you."

My nervousness turns to joy at the sight of Yolanda. She comes to the door in a yellow dress that looks like a cloud of light. Her smile makes me forget there's anyone else in the world besides us two.

"Daddy, this is Walter," she says. "Remember? I told you I have a date tonight."

"A date? Oh, yeah. I musta forgot," he says. But I can tell he didn't forget at all. He was just hoping I wouldn't show up.

Yolanda holds the door open for me. I step inside.

"Walter Davis," I say, holding out my hand to her dad.

"Parnell Jefferson," he says. His hand makes mine look like a child's. I try not to wince as he crushes it.

"So, what do you do, Walter?" he asks.

"I work in finance," I say.

"Oh, yeah? What firm?"

"I'm, uh...between positions at the moment."

Mr. Jefferson looks unimpressed. But I'm saved when someone else walks into the room.

"Oh, Yolanda, who this handsome young guy! What a nice suit he wear!"

I turn to see a tiny Chinese lady. I'm not tall, but she only comes to my chest. She's smiling so hard her face has disappeared in a mass of friendly wrinkles.

Yolanda rattles something off in Mandarin to her mother. She bows to me. I bow back.

Out of nowhere, I remember learning a single phrase of Mandarin from a movie I saw a long time ago. It's *Nǐ hǎo ma*, which means "How are you?" I decide to bust it out. Why not? When you have nothing to lose, you're not afraid to try anything.

So I bow again and say, "Nǐ hǎo ma?"

You would think I just grew a pair of wings. Her mom's eyes get big.

"I like this boy!" she says. "He okay!"

Yolanda laughs. She kisses her mom and dad good night and puts her arm in mine.

"Not too late, right?" says Mr. Jefferson.

"You be quiet!" says Mrs. Jefferson, hitting him on the arm. "She big girl now."

"Good night, Mom and Dad," says Yolanda.

We walk out the door together.

CHAPTER FOUR

For our first date, I decide it would be a good idea to go to a Chinese restaurant. That shows I'm interested in Yolanda's heritage and open-minded enough to try new kinds of food. So we go to a little place I found earlier. Nice, clean, but not too pricey.

The owners look at us strangely. I guess you don't see too many black people in Chinese restaurants. But they lighten up when Yolanda starts talking to them in Mandarin. Next thing you know, we've got three waiters swarming around us. They treat us like royalty.

"Wow," I say. "I need to learn how to speak more of that."

"You really impressed my mother," she says. "Where did you learn how to say nǐ hǎo ma?"

"Oh, I picked it up in my world travels," I say. Then I wink to show I'm joking. She laughs again. It sounds like a handful of silver coins jingling. I could tell jokes all night just to hear that laugh.

I let Yolanda do the ordering. A waiter brings a vase for the flowers I stole. We sit and smile at each other. I hope they take a very long time to bring our food. I want this night to go on forever.

"Well, looks like your dad already hates me," I say.

"Oh, don't worry about him," Yolanda says. "He's just being protective of his little girl."

"How did your parents meet anyway?"

"Dad's a minister. He was a missionary in China. He met Mom while he was working over there. I know, they look kind of funny together, right?"

"As long as they're happy," I say.

"Well, they're good people, but I can't wait to move out and get my own place. They're letting me stay with them until I save up enough money. Where do you live, Walter?"

"Oh, I, uh...I have a small place downtown," I say. I glance out the window at my car. "A *really* small place. So, what kind of plans do you have for the future?"

Yolanda shrugs. Our drinks come. Hers has a little paper umbrella in it. She takes it out and plays with it.

"I'm not sure yet," she says. "I like my job for now, but I definitely want to go back to school. I just don't know what I want to study. Maybe business. What about you?"

"I got my associate degree in business admin last year," I say. "So I've been looking like crazy for a job. No luck yet."

"Things are tough out there, aren't they?" says Yolanda.

"You know it."

Our food comes. There are about ten different dishes. Everything smells so good that I forget to worry about how much it's all going to cost. I let Yolanda tell me what everything is, even though I can't understand half of it.

I eat as slowly as I can. I'm having the time of my life. I have just one regret. I wish Moms was still around, so she could meet Yolanda. She would have liked her.

Finally, we finish eating. The waiters bring fortune cookies on little plates.

"I love these things," I say.

"You know these aren't really Chinese, right?" Yolanda says. "They were invented here, in this country."

"They're still fun," I say. "As long as you remember not to take them too seriously."

We open ours at the same time. I read mine, then look over at her. Her face has a funny expression on it.

"What's yours say?" she asks.

I show her: *You will be a great success in business.* Just what I wanted to hear.

"What about yours?" I ask her.

But she shakes her head primly. Then she folds up her fortune and puts it in her purse.

"You're not gonna tell me?" I say. "Is it that bad?"

"No, not bad," she says, smiling. "Just... personal."

"Are you ever gonna show me?"

"Maybe someday," she says. "But not today."

Finally, the waiters clear the last crumb off the table, and the owners start clearing their throats. I look at my watch. It's ten o'clock. I can't believe it. We've been sitting here for almost three hours.

"I better get you home," I say.

I call for the bill. I don't want to look at it, but I have to. I try not to wince. Eighty-nine dollars. Oh, well. I'd gladly pay ten times that for a date with this African-Chinese princess.

We bow our way out the door, thanking the owners for everything. Then we head back to her house. It's a beautiful night. We leave the car windows open, so we can feel the breeze.

Soon we pull up outside her house. I leave the car running and the lights on. I don't want her dad to think I'm getting any ideas.

"Well, thanks for a great time," Yolanda says.

"Me too," I say. "I really mean it. I had a blast."

We look at each other for a long moment. Then the porch light comes on. Mr. Jefferson appears in the doorway.

"Oh, are you home already?" he calls. "I was just doing a security check."

"Daddy and his security checks," Yolanda says.

"I guess this kills any chance of a good-night kiss," I say.

I'm just joking around, but Yolanda looks at me, half smiling and half serious.

"There's always next time," she says.

And I can tell she means it.

I walk her to the door and say good night. I make a point of looking her dad in the eye and shaking his hand again. Then I get back in my car and take off.

I keep driving until I'm at the city limits, near a quiet park. Here I pull over. I get my blanket and pillow out of the trunk. Then I crawl into the backseat. It's been one of the best nights of my life. I feel like a king.

The last thing I do before I fall asleep is touch the wad of cash in my pocket. It helps remind me that everything really is going to be all right...someday.

CHAPTER FIVE

I wake up later than I meant to. All the excitement from last night wore me out, I guess.

Right away, I can tell something is wrong. But I'm so sleepy I can't tell what it is.

Then it hits me. The world has gone sideways. And my car is moving.

I sit up in the backseat. The front of the car is tilted up. And in front of it is a tow truck.

I'm so sleepy, it takes me a minute to figure out what's going on.

I'm getting towed.

I climb into the front seat and start leaning on the horn. After a minute, the truck slows down. Before it even stops, I'm out the door. I trip and fall on the road. Great. Now my pants have stains on the knees. I get to my feet as the driver gets out of the truck.

"Man, what are you doing?" I say. I'm trying not to yell, but I'm as mad as they come.

"What are *you* doing?" he says. He's a big greasy guy with a beard. His T-shirt doesn't even cover his belly. I guess some people get dressed without looking in a mirror.

"You're not supposed to tow cars with people in them," I say.

"Yeah, well, you're not supposed to park in tow zones," he says.

"I didn't know it was a tow zone. Didn't you see me back there?"

"All I saw was a blanket. How was I supposed to know there was a person under there?"

"Well, you know now. So how about you cut me loose?"

He crosses his arms and shakes his head.

"You been towed," he says. "That's it. You want your car back, you gotta come down to the impound lot. Or pay me right here."

"Pay you? How much?"

"Two hundred and seven dollars."

"What? That's robbery!"

"That's what it costs."

"What gives you the right to charge me money for my own car?"

"I got a contract with the city," he says. "That's what gives me the right. That's the way it works."

There's no way I can afford to part with that much money. I decide to come clean with the guy. I hope he takes pity on me.

"Look, man," I say. "Two hundred bucks is practically all I have. I can't afford that. And I need this car. I...I live in it. I got nowhere else. Times are tough. This is my home right now."

I was hoping he would understand. But when he hears I'm homeless, that seems to make things worse. It's like a magic word in reverse. When somebody hears it, they harden their hearts against you. It's like you've got a sickness, and they don't want any part of it.

"Pay me, or I'm rolling," he says.

There's no way I can do it. So I ask him to wait while I take my toiletry bag out of my car. The rest of my stuff is already at the bus station. At least I don't have to carry it all.

"When you come up with the cash, you can have your car back," says the driver. He gives me a card with the address of the impound lot on it. "There's a daily storage fee.

The longer you leave it, the more it's gonna cost you."

"Great," I say. "Nice to meet you too."

Then I watch as my car disappears down the road.

It's a long walk back to the city. By the time I get downtown, it's nearly nine o'clock. I decide to go straight to the postal center. For the first time, I hope Yolanda isn't there. I'm ashamed to see her right now. I don't want her to see the defeat on my face.

But she's behind the counter, talking to someone. When I see her through the window, I almost turn and walk away. But she's already seen me. So I go in, acting like everything's fine, and shoot her a smile. She smiles back. At least she's too busy to talk.

I check my mailbox. Nothing.

Then I go to the computer and check my email. There's a message for me:

Dear Mr. Davis,
We would be happy to give you an interview.
Please come by today at 3:00 PM.
Sincerely,
Capital Investments, Inc.

Capital Investments is one of the new firms in the financial district. They have offices in a beautiful building with gold windows. I haven't done too much research on it yet. But it looks like a multimillion-dollar corporation.

And they want to talk to me.

Suddenly my whole day has changed. I clap my hands and pump my fist in the air.

"What are you so happy about?"

I turn to see Yolanda smiling at me. Her customer has left. I jump up and smile back.

"Just a little piece of good news," I say. "Could be a good lead."

"That's nice. Haven't you been to bed yet?"

"What do you mean?" *Uh-oh*, I think. *Can she tell I slept in my car?*

"You're still wearing your suit," she laughs. "And your knees are dirty."

I look down. There are soiled patches on my pants, where I hit the ground when I fell out of the car.

"Oops," I say. "Yeah, I was up late."

"Doing what?"

"I was, uh…praying. Thanking God for such a wonderful date last night."

"For real, Walter?" She looks like she doesn't know whether to believe me or not.

"Yeah. And I was also praying that if I asked you out again, you would say yes."

Uh-oh, I say to myself. *You better shut up. You don't have a car anymore.*

But I can't help myself. She's so beautiful. And I like her so much. All I want is to be with her. It comes out of my mouth before I can stop it.

She's still smiling. She thinks I'm funny.

"Why do you wear that suit all the time?" she says.

"Well," I say, "it was a present from my mother. And she used to say that the world judges a man by how he looks. So I always try to look my best."

Yolanda nods.

"I always felt like it was more important what you have inside," she says.

"That too," I say. "But people don't give you a job just because you're a nice person. You have to look the part."

She laughs again.

"Walter, I would love to go out with you again," she says.

"Great. What about tonight?"

"I can't make it tonight. But I'm free tomorrow night."

"Tomorrow night it is," I say.

How you going to pick her up, fool? says a voice inside my head.

But I'll worry about that later. Right now I have an interview to get ready for.

CHAPTER SIX

From the postal center, I head straight to the bus station. There I change into jeans and a T-shirt. I grab my copy of *Seven Habits*. Then I take my suit to the dry cleaner's, which is just around the corner. They tell me it's going to be a while.

I have nowhere else to be, so I go outside to wait. I lean against the wall and start re-reading *Seven Habits*. This book has all the secrets I need to know to make it in business. I want to master all of them.

"How's it going, Walter?"

I look up. There's a bum sitting against a building, about twenty feet away. He's got a sign that says *HOMELESS—PLEASE HELP*. In front of him is an empty hat. At first I think he's just some panhandler. But then I realize I know this guy.

"Hey, Scooby," I say. "It's going great. How are things?"

When I first lost my place, it was too cold to sleep in my car. So I spent a couple of weeks in a shelter. It was not an experience I care to repeat. But Scooby and I got to know each other there. He's a good guy. Maybe forty years old. Not very clean, and he looks sick all the time. But he's friendly. And smart.

"Business is terrible," he says. "This economy is in trouble. Nobody has an extra cent these days. And all the Ponzi schemes in the news are making things worse."

I go over and sit down next to Scooby.

"What's a Ponzi scheme?" I ask.

"It's a kind of scam. It's when investors promise people really high returns that they can't deliver. It's a con game."

"I didn't know anything about that," I say.

"Let me tell you something, Walter," says Scooby. "In the world of finance, if something sounds too good to be true, it probably is."

"How do you know all this, Scooby?"

"I used to be in business. I had five convenience stores. And two houses. But I lost everything."

"How'd you do that?" I'm amazed. *If I ever got that far ahead*, I think, *the last thing I would do is lose it all.*

"I borrowed too much," he says. "I thought the economy would keep going up forever. But when things started heading south, I lost everything. We call that being over-leveraged."

41

I feel like I ought to be taking notes. Scooby knows a lot more than I realized.

"Say, Walter," says Scooby, "I'm pretty hungry. You wouldn't have a few bucks you could give me, would you? I can pay you back when things pick up."

I know Scooby isn't a drunk or a drug addict. He really will spend the money on food. So I reach into my pocket to peel off a few small bills. But then I remember I've changed my pants. My money isn't in my jeans. It's with my suit. How could I have forgotten that?

"Scooby, I'll be right back," I say.

I run to the dry cleaner's. The lady who owns it happens to be Chinese too. Her name is Mrs. Wong. She listens to my story. Then she tells me she didn't see my money. I can tell she's being honest. Sometimes you just know about people. She lets me search through my pants. She even lets me look around the floor of her shop.

42

Nothing.

My money is gone.

Okay, Walter, think. Think hard. Where did you last see the money?

I remember. Last night, as I was falling asleep, I felt it in my pocket. I had it then. So it must have fallen out in the car.

Which is now at the impound lot.

I debate calling the lot to ask them to look for it. But that has to be the stupidest idea I've ever had. Of course they'll find it. Then they'll keep it.

Because that's the way it works.

How can I even pay for my suit? Mrs. Wong is waiting to see what I'm going to do. She reminds me of Yolanda's mom. I wonder if I can get lucky twice in a row. What do I have to lose?

I bow deeply. Then I say, "Nǐ hǎo ma?"

Her face lights up, and she laughs.

"Where did you learn that?" she asks. "Black people don't speak Mandarin!"

43

You need to meet Yolanda, I think.

But that's too complicated to explain right now. Instead, I tell Mrs. Wong about my job interview. I tell her what happened to my money. I beg her to let me pay her later. She nods. I've been in here before. She knows me well enough.

"You can pay later, okay," Mrs. Wong says. "I remember your face."

"Thank you, thank you, thank you," I say.

Mrs. Wong smiles again.

"In Mandarin, we say 'Xiè xiè,'" she says. It sounds like *sheh sheh*.

"Xiè xiè," I say, and I bow again. That information might come in handy. It would sure impress Yolanda's mom.

My suit is ready. I put it on in the washroom at the bus station. It looks great. Mrs. Wong even got the dirt out of the knees.

Then I head for Capital Investments. It's almost three o'clock. I'm so worried about my money I feel like I'm going to throw up. But I can't show that now. I need to put my game face on.

Finally, I have a real job interview.

It's time to show the world who Walter Davis really is.

CHAPTER SEVEN

"**N**ow that is the sharpest suit I have seen in a while."

The man who's speaking is just a few years older than me. He sits in a black leather office chair. He's blond, trim, with ice-blue eyes. He stares at me for a full five seconds. Like he's waiting for me to crack. I look back at him. Maybe he thinks he can make me nervous. And to tell the truth, I'm terrified. But I'm not going to show it.

"Thanks," I say. "I like yours too."

He smiles. Then he holds out his hand.

"Jon Watts. You can call me Jonny."

"Walter Davis." We shake.

"So, you want to work for Capital. What do you bring to the table?"

"I'll be straight with you," I say. "I don't have a fancy education. What I do have is brains and talent. And I can work harder than anyone. If you give me a chance, I won't let you down."

Jonny nods. Then he smiles.

"Let's take a walk," he says.

We go down a hallway lined with office doors. Then we come to a big room with lots of desks in it. On every desk is a phone. And on every phone, someone is talking a mile a minute. They're mostly men around my age. A few women. A few older guys.

"This is the boiler room," says Jonny. He steers me to an empty desk. Then he pushes a phone at me. "This is yours," he says. He hands me a couple of papers. "This is your script. Here's a list of numbers. You want people to invest with our company.

47

Tell them anything you want. I don't care. Just get their money. Once they say yes, pass them on to a supervisor. We'll get their personal information. All you have to do is sell. You follow me?"

I nod. Seems simple enough.

"All right," says Jonny. "Go ahead and dial that first number."

I dial. An old lady answers.

"This is Walter with Capital Investments," I say, reading from the script. But the words run together in my head. I can't think. I toss the script aside and speak from the heart. "Can I talk to you about your future?"

"Well, I suppose so," says the old lady on the other end.

I don't even remember what happens next. We talk for about five minutes. At the end of it I've promised her 30 percent returns in the next year. And she's agreed to invest ten thousand dollars with Capital Investments.

I hang up the phone. Jonny's eyes are huge. He starts to clap.

"Let's hear it for Walter!" he shouts. "On the job five minutes, and already he brings in ten large! Give it up, boys!"

The room breaks into applause. Guys I don't know are standing up, yelling my name. It's all pretty overwhelming. Jonny holds my hand up like I've just won a fight.

"Walter," says Jonny, "you just got yourself a job."

"Thank you," I say. "Thank you. Thank you."

I'm still saying thank you in my head an hour later, as I'm walking out of town. I'm headed for the impound lot, where my car is. If I can talk an old lady into investing ten thousand of her hard-earned dollars, I can talk some yahoo into letting me look inside my own car for five minutes.

Which I do.

I tear the car upside down. But the money isn't there.

"Did you go through my car?" I ask the guy behind the counter. He's not the guy who towed me. He's even greasier and hairier. *Must be the owner*, I think.

"We don't go in the cars, man," he says. "What do you think I am, a thief?"

"You stole my dang car, didn't you?" I say.

"The law is the law, my friend," he says. "That's the way—"

"I know, don't tell me," I say. "That's the way it works."

I've got nothing else to do, so I head for the part of town where I got towed. I know it's a long shot, but I have to check. It takes me an hour to walk there. I scan the ground for a wad of cash.

Yeah, right. Like someone is going to leave something like that just laying there. If this is where I dropped it, it's long gone.

No use crying over spilled milk. I console myself by pretending a widow found my money. A widow with nine starving children. She needed the money worse than I did. That's why this happened. It helps me feel a little better. But not much.

I head back to the city. My watch tells me it's going on six o'clock. The shelter opens at eight. I have two hours to kill. I walk slow, taking my time. It's a nice night. The whole way, I think about Yolanda. How she looked last night, and how she smelled. How close I came to kissing her. If not for her dad in the doorway, that is.

That's all right. If I had a daughter, I'd be protective too. I kind of like old Parnell. You have to respect someone who protects the people he loves.

I go to the bus station and change into jeans and a T-shirt. I put my suit away as carefully as possible. Then I go to the shelter to get in line. It's easy to get a bed on warm nights like this. It's harder in the middle of winter, when not getting a space means you could die.

The shelter is hard to sleep in. The blankets and pillows smell terrible. There's always someone raising a fuss. Crying, yelling, coughing, shouting. Always something. You learn to tune it out after a while.

Besides, I have tomorrow to look forward to. My first day on the job.

I won't be homeless much longer.

CHAPTER EIGHT

I'm up bright and early for my first day at work. To tell the truth, I didn't sleep a wink. I was too nervous and excited. And the shelter is just too loud. But being tired is nothing. I'd swim through a river of razor blades for a shot at a job. And now I've got one. Nothing, and I mean nothing, is going to slow me down.

I'm at the bus station just after sunrise. I get out my suit and put it on. It's a little wrinkled, but I've already made my first impression. And it was a good one. Today is not about appearances. It's about results.

Can I do better today than I did yesterday? Of course I can. I have to. That's the key to success.

I eat a breakfast burrito at my regular place. Then I start heading for the office. My office. My job. It feels so good to think that, I say it out loud. I don't care who hears me talking to myself. I have a job.

"You hear that, Moms?" I whisper. "I'm gonna make you proud."

I'm coming up on the block where Capital's offices are. Something seems to be going on today. There's a big crowd of people standing outside the building. Probably shooting a movie, I think. They do that a lot in this city.

I push my way through the crowd up to the front. But I don't see any movie cameras. All I see are a couple of cops standing guard at the front door. I've never been in trouble with the law, but I do know that cops never mean good news. Something bad is going down.

I nudge the guy next to me.

"Hey, what's going on?" I ask.

He looks at me. "Haven't you heard?"

"I haven't heard anything. What's up?"

"You work here?" he says.

"I work at Capital. Today's my first day."

"Well, I'm sorry to tell you this, buddy," says the guy. "But your first day is also going to be your last."

I feel like the ground is falling away from me. I'm in shock. I stagger, then catch myself.

"What do you mean?" I ask.

"Two words, pal," says the guy. "*Ponzi scheme*."

Ponzi scheme? *You have to be kidding me*, I think. This is just what Scooby was talking about. People taking other people's money. Pretending they'll get great returns. But really, all they get is robbed.

What else did Scooby say? If something sounds too good to be true…then it probably is.

Suddenly it hits me. I robbed an old lady yesterday.

"Here they come!" someone else yells.

At that moment, the front door opens. There are a lot of cops, and a lot of guys in suits. One thing I notice right away is that the guys in suits are in handcuffs. Some of them are trying to hide their faces.

Then I recognize Jonny Watts. He's got handcuffs on too. His cocky attitude is gone. He looks like he wants to cry.

I know how he feels.

"You got to be kidding me," I say.

"Sorry, bro," says the guy I was talking to. "Heck of a way to start your first day."

The guys in suits are being loaded into cop cars. But I can't watch anymore. I find a bench and sit down.

Scooby was right. Corruption is everywhere.

Who was I kidding? I thought I could make it in the world of high finance. But the only firm that would give me a chance turned out to be crooked.

I put my head in my hands. I don't belong in this city. I need to leave. Ever since Moms and I came here, I've had nothing but trouble. Little by little, everything has been taken away. I've lost it all. Home, car, money. Even my own mother was taken from me. And now I've lost the one thing I managed to hang on to all this time—hope.

That's it. I'm done. I'm out of here. I don't know where I'm going, but anywhere is better than here. I'll pawn my suit. I'll get my car back. I'll fill the tank with gas. And then I'll leave.

Suddenly I feel like a huge weight has come off my shoulders. I know this is the right thing to do.

I go back to the bus station for the last time. I put on my old clothes again. I fold up my suit. Then I go to the pawn-broker's place, just a few blocks away. I know Moms spent over four grand on the clothes and the briefcase. After a long argument, I get four hundred bucks for it all, plus a pawn ticket.

It breaks my heart to think of how hard Moms worked to buy this suit for me. All so I could get a good job. But I'm not going to stand here in a pawnshop and cry. I have a new plan already, and I'm going to follow it. That's one of the seven habits from my book. Know what you want and work for it. All I want right now is to get out of this town before it kills me.

I make the long walk back to the impound lot. I go to the counter and hand over most of the cash I just got. The guy behind the counter asks me to wait a minute while he finds his receipt book.

I don't care. What's my hurry? I have nothing but time.

CHAPTER NINE

After I pay my towing charge and the storage fees, I have eighty-one dollars left. That's enough to fill the tank with gas and buy enough food for a few days. And then what will I do? I have no idea. It's in God's hands now.

I never was very religious. But maybe I should start going to church. Nothing I do seems to work. And come wintertime, a nice warm church would be a good place to hang out.

Then I remember something. How could I have forgotten? I was supposed to have a date with Yolanda tonight.

Well, that's not going to happen now. I'm so depressed I can't even face her. What will I do? Just not show up, I guess. I hate doing that, but I can't look her in the eye and tell her I'm homeless. Unemployed. Broke. She would throw me out like last week's trash. And her dad would hold the door open for her.

It's not right to just blow her off. But it doesn't matter if I call her or stand her up. Either way, I lose her. And after what I've just been through, I can't take the idea of being humiliated again.

Today was supposed to be the best day of my life. Instead, it's one of the worst. I haven't felt this empty since I watched my mother pass away.

"Give me a second to find your keys," says the owner. He's looking around behind the counter. "It's a little crazy here this morning. The courier is late again."

"Sure," I say. "Take your time. I got nowhere to be."

The owner goes to the door and opens it.

"Steve!" he yells. "That courier come by yet?"

I can't hear Steve's answer, but it must be bad news. The owner slams the door and shakes his head in disgust.

"People are so unreliable," he says to himself. Then he picks up a newspaper and looks under it. My keys are underneath. "Here are your keys, sir. Sorry to keep you waiting."

I take my keys. But I don't leave just yet. A lightbulb has gone off in my head.

"You say you're waiting for a courier?" I ask him.

"Yeah, that's right. I have a package that has to go across town. And it needs to be there in an hour."

"You mind me asking how much they charge you for that?"

"Thirty-five dollars."

I nod.

"I'll do it for twenty," I say.

"What? Are you serious?"

"Give me the package, and I'll deliver it right now. Twenty bucks. Guaranteed."

"How do I know you won't steal it?"

I take out my wallet. I remove my driver's license and put that in my shirt pocket. Then I hand my wallet over to him.

"Here," I say. "That's everything I have. All my ID, my money, everything. When I come back, call them up and ask if they got the package all right. Then you pay me and give me my wallet back."

The owner stands there staring at me for a minute. I think he's about to throw me out. But then he nods.

"You got yourself a deal," he says.

I hold out my hand. We shake.

"I won't let you down," I say.

The package is a manila envelope. It feels like it's full of papers. I take it under my arm. Then I go out to the lot and find

my car. It starts up right away. That's something to be happy about, at least. If I had
engine trouble, I might just have to lie
down and die on the spot.

Then I drive across town. It feels good
to have my wheels again. I find the address
with no trouble. It's a law office downtown.
I know this city like the back of my hand.
That's one good thing about all the time
I spent job hunting.

I drop the package off. Then I head
back to the lot.

Back in the office, the owner is waiting
for me when I come in.

"I already called them," he says. "They
said you made the delivery. Nice work.
Here's your wallet back. And here's twenty
bucks."

He hands me a crisp new bill. I put it
in my wallet, along with the cash I have
left. It's a lot more fun putting money into
a wallet than it is taking it out. Now I'm

twenty dollars richer. Suddenly I don't feel quite so low anymore.

"Thanks," I say. "You going to have more packages to deliver?"

"I have to send one out every week," he says. "They're legal documents. Always to the same address. And they always need to be there by the same time. You think you can promise me that?"

"You bet," I say. "I'm never late. Guaranteed."

"Well, you just got yourself a job," says the owner.

"Mister," I say, "you have no idea how good those words sound to me right now."

CHAPTER TEN

Okay, so one little courier job a week is nothing. But ten of them…that would start to add up. A hundred, and I'd be in good shape.

It looks like I have a new job. And this one is *not* too good to be true.

It's just good.

It's two days later. I'm broke again. But this time it's okay. I just spent fifty bucks on a stack of business cards. I've never had business cards before. They make me feel official. But more importantly, they make me look good.

The business cards say *NEV-R-LATE URBAN COURIER*. And they have my name and phone number on them.

The phone number belongs to the new cell phone I just got. That's what I spent the rest of my money on. Can't do business if you don't have a phone.

So now I'm walking door to door. I go into every business I see. Lawyers, doctors, dentists, financial firms. I don't care. Everyone needs a courier sometime. And I want that courier to be me.

I do the same thing in each place. I introduce myself to the receptionist. I hand her a card and explain who I am. Then I ask if the office manager is available. Most of the time, the answer is no. But sometimes I get to speak to the person in charge.

"I'll make this fast, because I know you're busy," I say to them. "I can deliver anywhere in the city for half the price of the competition. I'm never late. Guaranteed. If you want a reference, call this number." And I give them the name and number of the owner of the impound lot. He's already agreed to be my reference. So maybe my car getting towed wasn't such a bad thing after all.

I've been doing this for a whole day. I've knocked on maybe fifty doors. I want to hit fifty more before five o'clock.

It's just three o'clock when my phone rings for the first time. I'm so excited, I almost drop it. A jeweler needs something picked up and delivered to him ASAP. Can I do it now?

"Sure thing," I say. "You'll have it in an hour."

While I'm making that delivery, the phone rings again. A music store owner needs me to go pick up a guitar for him. It just happens to be on the way to the jeweler.

"No problem," I say.

That's my first day. I make fifty bucks, cash. I charged the jeweler a little extra because it was a rush job. But he didn't care. He was just happy to get his package.

I sleep in my car again that night. But this time, I don't mind. I had enough money at the end of the day to buy a decent meal. And my brain is spinning with possibilities. How far can I take this thing? It's the right idea at the right time. I always thought I would love to work in finance. But it would be even better to work for myself.

I'm up bright and early the next morning. I grab a quick breakfast and start pounding the pavement again. Knocking on doors, introducing myself, handing out cards. I don't stop until lunchtime. My phone hasn't rung yet today, but I figure it will take time to build up a good business. I'm patient.

I keep going all afternoon too. By five o'clock my phone hasn't rung once. What's going on? It's the end of the day and I didn't get any work. What am I doing wrong?

I need more coverage, I realize.

Then I have another idea: Scooby.

Scooby isn't hard to find. He haunts the same turf day after day. If he's not on his regular corner, he's either at church or at the shelter. I track him down around six o'clock.

"Walter," says Scooby. "Nice to see you! How's it going?"

"Listen, Scooby," I say. "How would you like a job?"

His eyes get wide.

"A job? Seriously?" he says.

I explain what I'm doing. Then I tell him my offer: I'll pay him twenty bucks to deliver a hundred business cards for me.

Scooby smiles.

"I used to make two hundred grand a year," he says. "Now twenty bucks sounds like a fortune."

"Will you do it, Scooby?"

"Of course I will, Walter. It sounds perfect. If a man can't make a living, he has no pride. I was starting to get pretty depressed. You know what I mean?"

"Do I ever," I say. "You're going to need some clean clothes. I brought these for you." I give him my other pair of jeans and my last clean shirt. "Make sure you look presentable. Wash up and get a shave."

"No problem."

I give Walter the business cards. I even pay him in advance. Then we shake hands.

"If this thing takes off like I think it will," I tell Scooby, "there's a job in it for you. A real job. It will pay real money too. So don't let me down, Scoobs."

"I won't, Walter," he says.

I sleep like a baby that night, mostly because I'm so tired.

The next morning, I'm back at it. Knocking on doors, drumming up business. My phone rings at nine thirty. It's another job. I get two more jobs before lunchtime. I get four more in the afternoon.

At the end of the day, I've got one hundred thirty bucks in my pocket. And that's after I filled my tank with gas.

I go find Scooby again.

"I don't know what you're saying to people out there, but it works. You got me a lot of work today," I tell him.

"It's easy," he says. "If I'm talking to a woman, I just tell them you look like Tiger Woods. If it's a man, I tell them you're the next Donald Trump. Now everyone wants to meet you."

"Scooby, you just earned yourself a steak dinner," I say.

I treat us both at a steak house I know.

Last time I was here, it was with my moms.
We were celebrating my graduation from
community college. I try not to think about
that. It makes me too sad. Besides, I have
something new to celebrate.

After we've eaten, Scooby pats his
stomach and gives me a huge smile.

"Thanks, Walter," says Scooby. "I feel so
good, I hate to go back to that shelter."

"I know what you mean," I say.
"Hopefully you won't be living there too
much longer."

*And I won't be sleeping in my car much
longer either*, I think.

Scooby and I shake hands.

"You want to work again tomorrow?"
I ask him.

"You bet," he says.

"Great. I'll meet you at the shelter at
eight AM."

"I'll be there," Scooby says. "Wild horses
couldn't keep me away."

CHAPTER ELEVEN

Time is passing quickly now. A whole day will fly by without me even noticing. That's how busy I am. The phone just doesn't stop ringing. It turns out a reliable courier was just what this town needed.

Just two weeks have passed since I delivered that first package. In that time, I've earned over twelve hundred dollars. I gave Scooby a raise and bought him some new clothes. I bought clothes for myself too. But not a suit. People don't want a courier who looks slick. They want a guy who looks like he's not afraid to get his hands dirty.

So, I bought myself a uniform at a professional supply store. It's a dark blue jumpsuit with lots of pockets. I need the pockets because I have to carry a lot of things—a receipt book, an order book, a few pens and my cell phone, to name just a few. I even have a name tag that says *WALTER* in large red letters. Underneath that, it has the name of my business. People take one look at me and they know I'm serious. And that makes them trust me.

At the end of every day, I meet up with Scooby at a coffee shop. I got him a uniform too. So we sit in our blue jumpsuits and sip coffee. We talk about how things went that day and how we can do better. I've got Scooby delivering packages now too. He looks completely different. Even though he's still sleeping at the shelter, he looks full of pride. He got a haircut and some new glasses.

And now that he's eating regularly, he doesn't look sick all the time.

I'm still sleeping in my car. But now I'm just doing it to save money. Soon enough, I'll be able to get my own place again. I can't wait for that. I'll be off the street. And I am never, ever going back.

Now it's Monday, the start of my third week working for myself. I've been at it all morning. I'm sitting in my car, having a donut and taking a break. I'm in a part of town I know well. Across the street is the pawnshop where I sold my suit. And in my wallet is the pawn ticket.

I get out of my car and cross the street. In the window there are all kinds of things people have sold—a bowling ball, a computer, a tennis racket, a pair of earrings.

There's a mannequin too. And on the mannequin is my suit. At his feet is my Underwood briefcase. I never actually carried any papers in that thing. But it felt good to have it at my side. It made me look serious. Almost like a lawyer or something.

I take the pawn ticket out and look at it. Then I look up at the suit again. If I want it back, all I have to do is fork over four hundred bucks. Then it's mine again.

I think once more about how hard Moms worked to buy these things for me. All she ever wanted was to see me succeed. Part of me wants to buy it back just because it was a present from her.

But what would I do with it? The suit would just hang in my closet. I'd never wear it. The briefcase would just take up space. I don't need these things anymore. And if I hang on to that four hundred bucks, I'm that much closer to affording my own place again.

I remember what Yolanda said to me once. I told her the world judged a man based on his appearance. She said that what you have inside is more important.

I can see more than ever how right she was. I'm wearing clothes I wouldn't have been caught dead in a month ago. But I feel better than I've ever felt before. That feeling is something money can't buy. It's called self-respect.

I've been trying not to think about Yolanda. Ever since the night I stood her up, I've pushed her to the back of my mind. I haven't even been back to the postal center. It's just too painful to think of what I gave up.

Sure, we only had one date. I'm not saying I was in love with her. But she is definitely a special person. Someone I really would have liked to get to know. And who knows what might have happened down the road? We had a lot of the same goals. We could have made a good team.

I look at my reflection in the window of the pawnshop. What was I thinking by just not showing up for our date? That was the stupidest thing I could have done. I know I was afraid of losing her by telling her the truth about myself. But I should have tried anyway. There was a chance, no matter how small. She might have understood. But just blowing her off like that guaranteed I would have no chance at all. I acted like a loser.

That's it. I can't spend the rest of my life regretting one dumb move. Either I forget about her forever, or I make it right.

And I don't want to forget about her. Every time I think of how she looked that night, it's like a knife in my chest. That beautiful yellow dress, her deep, dark eyes, her gentle smile.

That's it. I've made up my mind. I'm going to her house tonight to apologize. Maybe she'll slam the door on me. Maybe her dad will break my neck. Well, maybe not. He is a minister, after all. But he's still a father. And fathers are protective of their little girls.

I have a long list of deliveries to make. After that, I'm going straight to her place. This might just be the scariest thing I've ever done. But it feels like the right thing too. She deserves an apology. And what happens next will be up to her.

CHAPTER TWELVE

That evening, I pull up in front of Yolanda's house. I park in the street. I don't even dare use the driveway. I sit there for a moment and look at the front door. I won't lie. I'm scared. Okay, not just scared. Terrified. But I know I have to do the right thing here. If nothing else, I need to let Yolanda know that I am sorry. So I get out of the car.

That walk to her front door? Now I know what a condemned man must feel on the way to his execution.

Parnell answers my knock. He stares at me like I'm a Martian.

"Can I help you?" he says finally.

"Hello, Mr. Jefferson," I say. "Is Yolanda home? There's something I need to say to her."

"Huh," he says. Parnell is holding a newspaper in one hand. As I watch, he rolls it up into a tube and uses it to smack his other hand. I wonder if he's thinking about hitting me with it. "And what would that be?"

"Ah, well," I say, "no disrespect intended, but I want to say it to her."

He looks at me for another few seconds. Then he nods.

"Okay," he says. Then he calls over his shoulder. "Baby! Someone here at the door for you."

"Who is it?" comes Yolanda's voice.

"You best come see for yourself," says old Parnell.

After the longest wait of my life, Yolanda comes to the door. She's only wearing jeans and a sweater, but she's still the most beautiful woman on the planet. I feel that knife in my chest again. Dang. I really screwed up.

"You gotta be kidding me," she says. "You?"

"Hello, Yolanda," I say.

"I'll be in the living room," Parnell says. He goes back into the house. But I can still see his shadow on the floor. He's hiding around the corner. I'm sure he's going to hear every word of this.

"Who that at the door?" I hear Yolanda's mom ask.

"It's that Davis character," Parnell says.

"Oh," says Mrs. Jefferson. Then she gets real quiet. Great. So they're both listening.

"Walter," Yolanda says, "what happened to you? We had a date. You stood me up."

"I know. I'm here to apologize," I say.

"Well, you better be," Yolanda says, putting one hand on her hip. "First off, I was worried. I thought something happened to you. You just dropped off the face of the earth. You haven't even been in to check your mail. I thought about calling the police to report you missing!"

"I wasn't missing," I say. "Something happened. Something I need to explain."

"Well, I'm not sure I even want to hear it," says Yolanda.

"I can't wait to hear it!" says Parnell from inside the house.

"Shh!" says Mrs. Jefferson.

"Yolanda," I say, "is there any chance we can talk somewhere a little more private?"

"Uh-uh," she says. "You got something to say, you say it. Unless you're ashamed of yourself."

I take a deep breath.

"Well, I am ashamed of myself," I say. "I just wanted to let you know something.

The reason I didn't show up that night is because my car got towed."

"That's it? That's your excuse?"

"No," I say. "It's more complicated than that."

"Walter, what are you talking about?" says Yolanda.

Here's the part where I should tell her I'm homeless. But I can't make myself say it. I'm too ashamed. Or maybe too proud. Whatever. The words just won't come out of my mouth. So I keep blathering.

"Well, first I lost my car, and then I lost all my money. It was my own fault. I'm not blaming anyone else. I was desperate. I couldn't even afford to buy you a milkshake. I thought about coming to tell you, but I was afraid of how you might look at me. Kind of like you're looking at me right now."

"So you decided you would just leave me waiting rather than be honest?"

"I'm so sorry," I say. "I wasn't thinking straight. I was having a really hard time. But things are different now. I've started my own business. It's going really well too."

"Well, I'm very happy for you," says Yolanda. "Is that it?"

"Yes," I say. "Wait. I haven't really apologized yet. I just want to say I know I messed up. So I came here to tell you, from the bottom of my heart. I am really, truly, deeply sorry. You deserve better than that. But I couldn't go another day without telling you how I feel. I think you're wonderful, Yolanda, but I understand if you never want to see me again."

"Are you done now?" she says.

"Yeah," I say. "I'm done."

"Well, you know something, Walter?" says Yolanda. "I do deserve better than that. So goodbye."

I swallow hard.

"Goodbye," I say.

She closes the door in my face. I turn around and head back to my car. I keep hoping I'll hear her door open again. Maybe she'll call out to me. Tell me she understands. That it's okay. We can work it out.

But she doesn't.

I start up my car and drive away. I feel like I just left a piece of myself behind.

CHAPTER THIRTEEN

Another night trying to sleep in the back of my car. Another night of no sleep. All I can think of is the way Yolanda was looking at me. I could see the hurt in her eyes. How could I have screwed up so badly? She was the one thing in my life that was going right, and I had to mess it up. I really must have something wrong with me.

And now she never wants to see me again.

It is a lonely sunrise.

After breakfast, I decide I need to forget about Yolanda. I really have no choice. It's either that or spend the rest of my life regretting a stupid mistake. You just have to move on sometimes, no matter how lousy it makes you feel.

So it's time for me to put the next phase of my plan into action.

I drive to the shelter where I've stayed many a night. Just walking in the door is depressing. The place reeks like a barn. But I remind myself that I'm not here to stay. I'm here for a higher purpose.

I say hello to the man working the reception desk. Then I go in to the main area, where about twenty people are having breakfast. The food smells and looks terrible. But it's all some people have to keep from starving to death.

"Hey, everybody," I say. "Can I have your attention, please?"

Some people ignore me. They think I'm just one more crazy person. Homeless shelters are full of them, after all. But others look at me curiously.

89

"My name is Walter, and I'd like to offer you some work," I say. "Would anyone like to earn twenty bucks today?"

Several hands go up right away. Others don't. You would think that everyone would want to work. But some people are here because they're mentally ill, or too sick or too old to work. People don't become homeless by choice. I've heard enough stories to know that all it takes is a series of bad breaks. Just like what happened to me. A lot of people have had even worse luck than I have. And imagine being sixty or seventy years old to boot. You can see how life just isn't fair sometimes.

But there are a number of younger healthy people who just need another chance. And I'm going to give it to them.

"Okay, everyone with their hands up, follow me," I say.

About ten people get up and follow me. We walk past the guy at the desk, whose jaw is hanging open.

"What's going on?" he says.

"It's a brand-new day," I say. "Opportunity just knocked for these people."

The guy smiles.

"Amen to that," he says.

Out on the street, I turn and wait for everyone to catch up. Then we walk in a group to the uniform supply store, just a few blocks away. I've already arranged with the owner of this place for a bulk discount. I buy ten T-shirts that say *NEV-R-LATE URBAN COURIER*. Then I have everyone put them on.

When that's done, I gather them all on the sidewalk. I hand each person a stack of a hundred business cards. I explain what I want them to do: walk around town and deliver these cards to businesses.

Everyone pick a different territory. Be polite. Be respectful. Get in and out, and don't waste anyone's time.

"Okay, that's your job," I say. "And to show you my heart's in the right place, I'm going to pay you half in advance. Here's ten bucks for each of you. Come back when you're done and I'll give you another ten."

I hand them each a ten-dollar bill. From the looks on some of their faces, you would think they just won the lottery. I figure maybe one or two of them will keep the money and throw away the cards. There's not much I can do about that. But most of them will do what I asked them to do. And they'll come back for more work again. Those will be my future employees.

"Now," I say. "Does anyone have any questions?"

"Yes, I have one," says a voice behind me. "Why did you make my little girl cry?"

For a moment, I don't even want to turn around. I know that voice. But I do turn. And who is standing there behind me but Parnell Jefferson.

"Mr. Jefferson," I say. "What are you doing here?"

"I decided to follow you last night," he says. "I know you slept in your car. And I followed you again this morning."

"You followed me?"

"I needed to know who was coming around my daughter," he says. "What's going on with you, Walter?"

That's it. No more hiding.

So I tell Mr. Jefferson everything. Including the fact that I'm homeless.

To my surprise, he listens. And nods. And when I'm done, he does something I wasn't expecting. He smiles.

"Thank you for being honest," he says.

"Mr. Jefferson, the last thing in the world I wanted to do was hurt your daughter,"

I say. "But I just couldn't stand the shame. I guess I'm a coward."

"No, you're not," he says. "Do you think you can be as honest with Yolanda as you just were with me?"

"Do you think she would listen?" I say.

"Well," says Mr. Jefferson, "there's only one way to find out."

"You mean I should go talk to her right now?"

"That's just what I mean. If you're serious about her, that is. If not, then don't bother."

"I just thought that after what happened yesterday—"

"Yesterday you told her half the truth," Mr. Jefferson interrupts. "What you need to do is tell her the whole truth."

I nod.

"You're right," I say.

"Well?"

"Is Yolanda at work right now?"

"Yes, she is."

"You want to walk with me?" I ask him.

"Sure, Walter, I'll come along," he says. "I'm dying to see how this turns out."

"So are we!" says one of my new employees. I'd forgotten about them. I turn and face them.

"Sorry, folks, this is some personal business," I say. "Meet me back here tomorrow morning to collect the rest of your pay. And I'll have more work for those interested."

"Good luck, Walter!" says a big guy with red hair. "Hope you work it out with her!"

"Yeah, good luck!" says everyone else. "Let us know what happens!"

"Thanks," I say.

Then Parnell and I head for the postal center. It's time to make things right for real.

CHAPTER FOURTEEN

M r. Jefferson says he'll wait outside while I go in. He doesn't want to interfere. So I head into the postal center by myself.

Yolanda is standing behind the counter. She's got a pile of rubber bands in front of her. She's sorting them according to color. There's nobody in line. It's just me and her. When she sees me, she stiffens up. A look comes over her face that tells me this is not going to be easy. Well, I didn't think it would be.

I walk up to the counter. She says nothing. She doesn't even look up. She just keeps sorting rubber bands.

"Hi," I say.

"Was there something I could help you with, sir?" she says.

"So it's like that?" I say.

"Yeah, it's like that," she says. "If there's nothing you need, I'm very busy right now."

"Yolanda, there's something else I have to tell you. I didn't give you the whole story yesterday."

She stops sorting the rubber bands and looks up at me.

"Oh, so you were lying?"

"No, I wasn't lying. I wouldn't do that to you."

"How do I know that? You stood me up with no trouble. Maybe you can lie just as easily."

Oh, boy. This is not going well. I can't believe how nervous I am. My palms are sweaty. I wipe them on my blue jumpsuit.

"Well?" she says. "What's this big thing you have to tell me? I don't have all day. These rubber bands are not going to organize themselves."

"Yolanda, the truth is, I'm homeless," I say. "And it's really embarrassing. So I didn't want you to know. I was afraid you wouldn't want to see me again. I stood you up because my life got turned upside down. Just when I thought I'd lost everything, I lost even more. When my car got towed, it meant I had to go back to the homeless shelter. I had no money. No job. No hope either. And I didn't want you to know how bad things were with me. I guess I was afraid. I'm sorry I didn't tell you the whole story. But now you know."

"I already knew you were homeless, Walter," says Yolanda.

I can't believe what I just heard. I stare at her, my jaw hanging open.

"What did you say?" I ask.

"Oh, come on. Give a sister some credit. The signs were all there."

"What signs?" I say. "I thought I was doing a good job of hiding it!"

"First of all, you wore the same suit every day," says Yolanda. "That was kind of a clue. Second of all, why would you come in here if you had a place of your own? You needed a mailbox because you needed an address to put on your résumé. Am I right?"

"You should have been a detective," I say.

"And another thing. You checked your email here all the time. Most likely, if you had a place of your own, you would have a computer too. But instead you used this one. So that was another clue."

"You should have been a *senior* detective," I say. "Anything else, Sherlock Holmes?"

"You did let a couple of hints drop," Yolanda says. "Like when we were out to dinner, you said you had a small place downtown. A really small place. You may not know this, but you looked out the window at your car when you said that."

"I did?"

"Yup. Body language is a dead giveaway."

"You're scaring me," I say. "So...you knew I was homeless, and you agreed to go out with me anyway?"

"Yes, I did."

"Why?"

Yolanda rolls her eyes.

"Do I really have to answer that one?" she says.

"What do you mean?"

"Walter, first of all, I knew enough about you to know that you're no bum. I could see how hard you were working to find a job. I know sometimes people just catch a bunch of bad breaks. That's not your fault. I knew you were the kind of guy who wouldn't rest until you'd gotten what you wanted out of life. And that made me respect you."

"Wow," I say. "I wish I had known that."

"Walter, what is wrong with you?" she says. "The fact that I went out with you wasn't enough to tell you how I felt? You think I just go out with any old guy who asks me? I'm very picky. Ask my parents. You're the first guy I've ever brought home to meet them."

"You're kidding me," I say.

"No, I'm not kidding," she says. "That's why it hurt me so bad when you didn't show up. I was beside myself, Walter. All I could think of was that you were hurt and couldn't get help."

"Yolanda," I say, "will you ever forgive me for being such an idiot?"

She gives me yet another long look. But this time, there's a tiny smile playing around her lips.

"Walter," she says, "go check your email."

"What? Why?"

"Because I sent you something."

"You sent me an email? How did you even know my address?"

Yolanda reaches under the counter and holds up a piece of paper. My résumé. It has my email address on it.

"When you came in to make copies of this, I made myself an extra one."

I'm amazed. "You did? But why?"

"I was curious to know more about you. Now, go check your email."

I go over to the computer and log in to my email account. I haven't checked it in a long time. There are a lot of messages. Some of them are from places I asked for a job, but I don't care about those anymore.

I keep looking through my inbox until I find a message from Yolanda. I click on it to open it up.

It reads:

Wherever you are, and whatever happened, it's okay. Just come back.

That's all it says. I check the message header to see when she sent it. The date is over two weeks old.

I get up and go back to the counter.

"You sent that before I even came back to apologize," I say.

"Believe me, there were times I wished I hadn't sent it. But now I'm glad I did."

"So am I," I say. "Thank you so much."

"You're welcome," she says.

"I…I don't know what to say."

"How about you tell me about this big business idea of yours, Mr. Urban Courier?"

"What? How did you know about that too?"

"It's on your name tag, genius," says Yolanda.

"Oh, right," I say. "I forgot. Listen... how about I tell you all about it over dinner tonight? If you'll give me another chance, that is."

CHAPTER FIFTEEN

Long story short…she gave me another chance. And this time, I didn't screw it up.

It's a year later. Yolanda and I are in the same Chinese restaurant we went to on our first date. But we're not eating. We're dancing. Lots of my old friends from the shelter are there. So are some of my best customers. All her family members are there too. Everyone is watching us dance. There's a DJ playing a Roberta Flack tune: "The First Time Ever I Saw Your Face."

Yolanda is wearing a white gown.

I'm in a tuxedo.

We just got married.

A lot's happened in a year. My business has grown. It's too big for me to run on my own anymore. I have twenty employees now. Most of them are people who used to be homeless and unemployed. Now they all have jobs. They can afford places of their own. They're off the street and supporting themselves. They're productive members of society. You can see the difference in the way they carry themselves. They feel alive again.

I have a new business partner too. She's the woman in my arms right now. Yolanda runs the administrative side of things. She takes care of the office. She's even got her own secretary to help her. Without her help, I'd be lost. She's smart and capable. She's my partner in every sense of the word.

I spend a lot of my time dealing with clients now. I still go around drumming up new business. But it's on a whole new level. Instead of knocking on doors, I sit in fancy boardrooms with executives of large corporations. I like it. It feels natural. Like it's what I was meant to be doing all along.

Scooby is still with me too. He's in charge of the employees now. He doesn't call himself Scooby anymore. Now he's back to calling himself Samuel. That was his name before he lost everything. He told me just the other day that he hasn't felt so good about himself in years. And he thanked me for giving him a chance. I told him he didn't have to thank me. He was helping me by doing such good work.

It makes me feel so good to look around the room at all these people. Parnell performed our wedding ceremony. I could see by the look on his face how proud he was that we were getting married. He's still protective of his little girl, of course. But it helps that he thinks a lot of his new son-in-law.

Mrs. Jefferson is standing next to him. If she smiled any harder, her face might fall off. She's been teaching me a lot of Mandarin. We can have a whole conversation now. She says I'm a natural. If we have kids, Yolanda and I want them to speak both languages.

And Yolanda wants kids. A lot of them.

I look down into Yolanda's eyes and smile.

"How you doing?" I ask.

"I'm great," she says. "How you doing?"

"Sorry I'm such a lousy dancer."

"That's okay. You're good at other things."

"Did I mention this is the happiest day of my life?"

"About a thousand times."

"Well, I'm going to say it again. In case you forget."

"I won't forget."

The song ends. Everybody claps. Then the DJ puts on some livelier music, and the floor fills up with people. Chinese, blacks, whites, Hispanics. It looks like the lobby of the United Nations. It's the oddest collection of people you'll ever see. And one of the happiest too.

Everybody starts to boogie like dancing is going out of style. The DJ switches back and forth, from soul and rap tunes to Chinese pop music to blues and rock and roll. Everyone is having such a good time that no one cares what they dance to. They just want to get down with their funky selves.

"By the way," says Yolanda. "I want to give you this."

She presses something into my hand.

"What is it?" I say.

"Just look at it," she tells me.

I open up my hand. It's a tiny piece of paper, all folded up. I unfold it. I can't believe my eyes.

"Is this what I think it is?" I ask her.

"Yes, it is."

"You saved it all this time?"

"I sure did. Read it."

It's the fortune from a fortune cookie. It's the one Yolanda got on our first date, in this very restaurant. The one she wouldn't show me that night.

The fortune says:

You will marry the man of your dreams.

"I thought you didn't believe in these things," I say.

"I never said that," she tells me. "I just said they weren't really a Chinese invention."

"How come you didn't show this to me before?"

"Because I didn't want to jinx it. I wanted it to come true," she says. "And it did."

I grab my wife close and hold her tight.

We're not rich. But we don't care about being rich. We just care about being happy. We don't have the money to go on a honeymoon right now. We don't care about that either. We'll spend tonight in a luxury hotel suite. We thought we would treat ourselves that much. Then it's back to our regular lives. That's okay. We love our lives just the way they are.

When we check out of the hotel, we'll go back to our new apartment. We just bought it a month ago. It's not a fancy place, and it's not very big.

But it's home.

The Way It Works is William Kowalski's second title in the Rapid Reads series. Kowalski is the award-winning author of four previous novels, including the international bestseller *Eddie's Bastard*. He lives on the South Shore of Nova Scotia with his wife and children.

RAPID READS

The following is an excerpt from
another exciting Rapid Reads novel,
The Barrio Kings by William Kowalski.

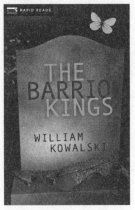

978-1-55469-244-6 $9.95 pb

"Look, man, real life is not always pretty.
Sometimes you gotta do hard things. You
have to protect what's yours in this life.
No one else will do that for you."

Rosario Gomez gave up gang life after his brother
was killed in a street fight. Now all he wants to do is
finish night school, be a good father and work hard
enough at his job at the supermarket to get promoted.
But when an old friend from the barrio shows up,
Rosario realizes he was fooling himself if he thought
he could ignore his violent past.

CHAPTER ONE

My name is Rosario Gomez. I'm twenty-three years old. I stock shelves at the supermarket downtown. I wear a tie to work every day, even though I don't have to. I wear a long-sleeved shirt to cover my tattoos. But I can't hide all of them. There's one on my right hand that says *BK* in small black letters. That one I can't hide. So I try to keep my right hand in my pocket when my boss is around.

My boss is Mr. Enwright. He's a fat, bald white guy who gets mad easy. But he's okay. Some of the other workers here call him Mr. Enwrong. I do not do that. Not to his face, and not behind his back. I need this job too bad. Enwright told me that once I get my GED he will promote me to assistant manager. That would be the most important job anyone in my family has ever had.

I was not always this straight. I came up rough. My neighborhood was on the news almost every night, and the news was never good. It was the kind of *barrio* nice people don't visit. There was nothing there for them. There was nothing there for me either. There was only survival, and I had to fight for that.

I dropped out of school to run with a gang called the Barrio Kings. I did some things I'm not proud of now. Like I said, I had to survive. I used to be the best street fighter around. I didn't like fighting. But I had no choice. I pretended to like it though. I used to smile. That scared people even more. And when you're scared, you lose.

Most fights are won before they start. You win them in your head, before you even throw a single punch.

I was just lucky that I was good at fighting, the way some people are just good at music or art. Sometimes I wonder if I should have been a boxer. But I always used to get this sick feeling in my stomach after I hit someone. It stayed with me. I don't miss that feeling. It's been a long time since I was in a fight. I hope I'm never in another one.

Things are different now. I've had this job for three years. I've stayed out of trouble. I don't go back to the old barrio anymore. I don't even miss it. Now I work from nine to five. After work, three days a week, I take the crosstown bus to the community college. That's where I take my night courses. I'm almost done with them. In just three weeks, I'm going to finish my high-school studies. Then I'll be the first person in my family to have a diploma too.

After class, I take another bus home. I live with my girlfriend, Connie. She's twenty. We've been together for two years. We're going to have a baby in a month. We already know it's a boy. We're going to name him Emilio. We have a crib all set up for him. We have a bunch of toys and clothes too. Connie's Aunt Carlita gave them to us. She has eight kids, so she has a lot of extra stuff.

By the time I get home after class, I'm wiped. But Connie has not been feeling too good lately, so usually I make dinner. I can't believe how big she is. Her feet hurt all the time. So do her hips and knees. I feel bad for her, but there's nothing I can do. And Emilio is almost here. I can't believe I'm going to be a dad.

Mr. Enwright told me that when I get that promotion, I will have to work longer hours, but I'll make more money. I can't wait. I have a plan. I'm going to save up money, and I'm going back to school. College this time. I'll take some business courses. I figure by the time Emilio is five, I can be a manager, and I will make even more money. That would put me on the same level as Mr. Enwright. I think Emilio will be proud to know his dad is a boss.

But I'm not stopping there. I want a business of my own. I don't know what kind yet. All I know is, I can see it in my head. Just like I used to see myself winning street fights. I can see myself in a three-piece suit. I'm not sitting in an office though. Who wants to sit still all day? Not me. I like to move around, talk to people, shake hands, make deals. I see myself in an airplane. I'm speaking different languages with people in other countries. Maybe I'll be selling things. Maybe I'll be setting up deals. Whatever it is, I'll be good at it. And I will make a lot of money.

But right now I need to come back down to earth. Mr. Enwright doesn't like it when people slack off. Not that I ever do. I just don't want to give him a reason to get mad at me. Not when everything is going so well.

Today is Thursday. That means I have class tonight. I hate riding that bus, but I can't afford a car right now. Cars are really expensive. You have your monthly payments, your insurance, your gas and repair costs. All that stuff adds up quick. And every penny I spend on a car means one penny less in the bank.

It doesn't matter about the bus. I don't mind. I do dream about a car though. I know just what kind I want. Not a low-rider, like I'm some kind of punk. I want a serious car. I want a black Lexus suv with a leather interior and tinted windows. I want people to look at that car and wonder who owns it. I want them to admire it. And it will have a nice stereo too. The kind you can hear a mile away.

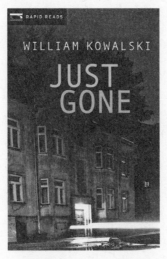

978-1-45980-327-5 $9.95 pb

With no one else to protect them, street kids welcome Jacky Wacky and his vigilante justice.

When Jamal and his sister, Chantay, arrive at Mother Angelique's inner-city homeless shelter, they are hungry and scared. Their mother is dead, and they are on their own. Angelique is fascinated by Jamal's stories of a man named Jacky Wacky, who protects the abandoned children of the city—and punishes those who harm them. A God-fearing woman, Angelique doesn't believe the stories at first. But strange things happen whenever Jamal is around, and she is ulti-mately forced to admit that the world may contain stranger truths than her faith can explain.

Tức quyết, tiếc nửa, tuyệt đối

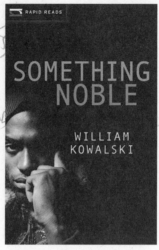

RAPID READS

SOMETHING NOBLE

WILLIAM
KOWALSKI

978-1-45980-013-7 $9.95 pb

What will it take to convince a drug-dealing gangbanger to donate a kidney to the dying half-brother he's never met?

When Linda learns that her son Dre needs a kidney transplant, her family's already shaky financial situation takes a turn for the worse. But when she discovers that the only one who can really help Dre is his half brother LeVon, a drug-dealing gang-banger, money is suddenly the least of her problems.